Build me a tree house,
With a ladder and swing,
We'll spend all day long,
Just doing our thing!

Build me a library,
With a roof made of glass,

We'll read lots of stories,
And watch stars shooting past.

Build me a castle,
With a tower so high,
We'll have a pet dragon...
To scare off passersby!

Build me a boat,
With a mast and a hold,
We'll be pirate children,
And find chests full of gold.

Build me a skyscraper,
With seven hundred floors.
We'll play hide-and-seek,
Behind all the doors.

Build me a submarine,
With gadgets galore.
We'll stop on the seabed,
And meet sharks, whales and more!

Build me a cabin,
With shutters and flowers,
We'll have great adventures,
In the mountains for hours.

Build me a rocket,
With beds that can fly,
We'll have so much fun,
Floating 'round in the sky!

Actually...
If I think very hard...

Build me a house,
With rooms big or small,
We'll all live together—
That's the best home of all.

Now, can you build a home for yourself or your bear?

Just start with a box,
or even some chairs,
Try under a table
covered with a sheet,
You could make it messy
or tidy and neat!
You need a way to get in
and a roof overhead,
You might want a cushion
to use as a bed,
Somewhere to peep out
and a flashlight for light,
A blanket to make it all cozy at night.